CLASSICS IN ACTION

TREASURE ISLAND

by Robert Louis Stevenson

Abridged by Rosalind Sutton

Illustrated by Eric F. Rowe

BRIMAX BOOKS · CAMBRIDGE · ENGLAND

At the Admiral Benbow

I am Jim Hawkins and my parents kept the inn, The Admiral Benbow at Black Hill Cove. I shall never forget the old seaman who came to stay with us, for that was the beginning of this story.

He was a tall, strong man; his hair hung in a greasy pigtail over his grubby blue coat; his nails were black and broken; but the most frightening thing about him was the sabre cut across one cheek. As he made for the inn another fellow followed behind, pulling an old sea-chest on a handcart. Looking round the cove, he whistled and sang to himself.

'Fifteen men on the dead man's chest – Yo-ho-ho, and a bottle of rum!'
That was his special song – one I came to know very well.

He rapped on the door demanding rum from my father and asking casually if we had many visitors. The answer, 'Very few,' seemed to please him and he decided to stay. ''I'm a plain man,'' he declared. ''Just bacon, eggs and me rum – that's all I need. Here, tell me when that is spent . . .'' and he threw down a few gold pieces . . . ''You can call me Captain.''

All day he'd wander round the

He stayed at the inn for months and my father, who had become very ill, could never pluck up courage to ask for payment. One late afternoon, Dr. Livesey called to see my father and then sat enjoying a smoke in the parlour. The Captain was drinking heavily and making a nuisance of himself. He even started up a quarrel with the doctor – threatening him with a knife. The doctor never moved – not a flicker.

"Put that knife away!" he ordered. "I am a magistrate. Any more trouble from you and I promise you shall hang at the next assizes." They glared at one another. Finally the seaman put up the blade and went back to his seat.

"And let me warn you, sir," went on the doctor, "rum is death to you. Keep off it and behave yourself."

The Captain held his peace and kept quiet for many nights afterwards.

cove, or up on the cliff with his brass telescope. He often asked if any seafaring men had passed along the road.

"See here, lad," he said one day. "Keep your eyes open for a seaman with one leg. Tell me at once. D'you understand? There's a silver fourpenny piece for you, every month, if you do as I say."

The very thought of that one-legged sailor haunted me, and in my dreams he became a terrifying monster.

Every evening the Captain would sit drinking strong rum, singing his song and telling blood-curdling stories of pirates and fights on the Spanish Main.

A visit from Black Dog

Meanwhile, my father grew weaker and mother was often upstairs looking after him. One morning, as I set the Captain's breakfast table, the parlour door opened and in stepped a stranger. He was pale, had two fingers missing from his left hand and wore a cutlass. I was always on the lookout for a sailor – this man had something of the sea about him. He ordered rum and questioned me about the table. "It's for a man staying here," I answered; "the Captain."

"My mate would likely be called 'the Captain' . . . Has a scar on one cheek . . . Let's say your Captain has a scar, eh? . . . Yes . . . Then your Captain is my mate, Bill . . . Where is he?" I glanced through the window. "He's out walking."

He kept looking out and when he saw the Captain returning he pulled me with him behind the open door.

In strode the Captain slamming the door shut. Then he spun round at the sound of the stranger's voice. "Well, now, Bill, you know me – your old shipmate!"

The Captain could only gasp: "Black Dog!"

"Who else?" laughed the stranger.

"All right," the Captain admitted. "You've run me down. what d'you want?"

9

"That's more like it, Bill. I'll have a glass o' rum and we'll talk, eh?" I served them and was ordered out. I couldn't hear their conversation, but gradually they became quarrelsome.

Suddenly, with clashing steel they were hard at it. Black Dog cried out and was running through the door, blood streaming from his shoulder. The Captain followed, cutlass raised and would have split his head in two, but our signboard swung and intercepted the blow. Black Dog disappeared. The Captain, dazed and bewildered, reeled back into the parlour.

"Rum," he kept saying. "Rum, Jim." I ran to get the drink – all thumbs I was. Then I heard a tremendous thud. There lay the Captain, full length on the floor. My mother came racing downstairs and we tried to raise his head. His breathing was loud and difficult; his face a terrible colour. How thankful we were when in walked Dr. Livesey.

"He's wounded!" we both cried. "Wounded? Fiddlesticks!" declared the doctor. "He's had a stroke – as I warned he would. Now, Mrs. Hawkins, you get back to your husband and keep all this from him. Jim, fetch me a basin and hold it while I take some blood from his arm." The doctor ripped the Captain's sleeve showing his arm covered with tattoo marks. One of these read: 'Billy Bones his fancy.' Sometime after being cut and bled, the Captain opened his eyes. "Where's Black Dog?" he cried.

"There's no Black Dog here," answered the doctor. "You've been drinking rum AND I warned you. Now Mr Billy Bones, one glass of rum won't kill you – but you won't stop at that – so, you'll die! Do you hear? Die! . . . Now, help us a little, and we'll get you upstairs."
Between us we got the Captain to his bed.

The black spot

Later, when I took up the Captain's medicine, he started getting excited, begging me for rum. I pacified him with just one glass.

"I must get away, Jim," he started. "They'll have the black spot on me. You saw Black Dog? . . . Well, there's worse than him. It's my sea-chest they're after. If I don't trick 'em, you get to that doctor o' yours, magistrates and such like – they'll catch 'em – all old Flint's crew – all that's left. I was Flint's first mate. I'm the only one as knows the place – give it me he did as he lay dying . . . But, listen, Jim, not a word unless they get the spot on me, or you see Black Dog again, or the one-legged man; yes, him above all."

"But what is the black spot, Captain?" I asked.

"A summons, mate . . . I'll tell you if they bring that. Keep your weather eye open, Jim. I'll share with you, equals, I swear . . ." He rambled on and then slept.

I had no time to worry about any of it, for that evening my father died. Our sorrow and all the arrangements to be made put the Captain right out of my mind.

The day after my father's funeral I stood at the door watching the swirling mist. Things appeared and disappeared as the fog covered or uncovered them. Suddenly, I heard a tapping noise and a tall black figure floated towards me. It was there; then it was not.

Was it a ghost? . . . I froze with terror and the icy air.

Nearer and nearer it came . . . Tapping! . . . Tapping! . . .

A blind man! . . . And deformed surely, hunched in his tattered cloak. A green shade hid his eyes and part of his face – a dreadful sight.

"Will any kind soul tell a blind man where he's at?" he called in a sing-song voice.

"You're at the Admiral Benbow, my good man, Black Hill Cove," I managed to answer.

"Ah, a young voice. Give me your hand, friend, and lead me in."

I held my hand out and the horrible, soft-spoken, eyeless creature gripped it like a vice. I tried to pull back but in one move he had me close. "Now, boy, take me to the Captain."

"I dare not, sir . . . The Captain's not well, he . . ." He wrenched my arm.

"March!" he ordered twisting my arm again. I led him in to the old buccaneer – sitting there in a daze of rum. He looked up and in one second was stark sober, but too weak to get up.

"Stay there, Bill," said the blind man. "Hold out your right hand . . . Now, boy, take his wrist and bring his hand to my right hand." In silence we both obeyed and I saw something pass into the Captain's palm. He closed his fingers. "That's done, then," said the blind man and with incredible speed he was out of the inn and tapping into the distance.

When we'd gathered our senses I let go his wrist and the Captain looked at the message.

"Ten o'clock!" he cried. "Six hours! We'll do them yet!"

He sprang to his feet, staggered and swayed, then with a choking sound crashed to the floor.

I ran to him; I called my mother; but the Captain was dead.

I had grown to pity the old buccaneer and feeling sad for him and my father, I burst into tears.

The sea chest

I told my mother everything I knew and we both realised that if those men returned we could be in great danger. I couldn't leave her alone so, we set out together to find help.

Beyond the cove lay a hamlet – just a few cottages. How thankful we were to see candlelight shining from the windows. Several men offered to ride for the doctor; but they were all too scared to come back to guard the Admiral Benbow. My mother was furious.

"You chicken-hearted lot!" she cried. "Jim and I will go on our own then. We'll open the chest and I'll take the money he owes us. Be so kind as to lend us a bag, Mrs Crossley."

They said we were fools but gave mother the bag and me a loaded pistol. One lad set out for the doctor.

The mist was clearing and the moon rising; we hurried along the hedges in silence. We heard nothing; we saw nothing; the inn door closed behind us. I slipped the bolt and we stood in the dark, breathless and alone with the dead body.

Mother lit a candle and I drew the blinds. There lay the Captain with a round piece of paper near his hand. It was black on one side and had writing on the other. It read: 'You have till ten tonight.'

The clock whirred and struck. Six o'clock! Would those men return at ten?

"The key, Jim," urged my mother. I searched his pockets – there were several oddments, but no key. I tore open his shirt. There it was on a tarry string.

Mother led the way with the candle and we hurried upstairs. There in his little room was the Captain's old sea-chest. She took the key – it fitted and turned. As she lifted the lid, out came a strong smell of tar and tobacco.

A good suit of clothes lay at the top; a quadrant and sticks of tobacco; two brace of pistols; a bar of silver; some trinkets, compasses and a few curious shells. Then came the last thing of all, an old cloak, white with sea stains and underneath this a packet of papers sewn up in oil-cloth and a canvas bag that jingled with gold.

"Hold this bag," said my mother and she started counting out from the sailor's bag into her own, determined to take the money owed to her. The candle flickered; I heard a tap – tap – tap! It was the blind man's stick on the frozen road. Then it struck the door; the handle grated and the bolt rattled. There was silence – inside and out.

At last the tapping started again – fading away to nothing. Mother, frightened though she was, continued to count out the coins. A low whistle came from away up on the hill.

"I'll settle for this!" she cried and was on her feet.

I grabbed the papers. "And I'll take these to make things even!" We groped our way out and were off. We heard footsteps running and behind us we saw a light swaying – they had a lantern.

My mother stopped, "Go on, Jim . . . take this . . . I'm going to faint!" We'd reached a little bridge when she fell on my shoulder. I dragged her down the bank and partly under the arch.

The last of the blind man

Our enemies were approaching the inn. I crawled back up the bank to watch.

There were three men, hand in hand – the middle one the blind beggar. Several others hesitated at the open door.

"IN! Get in!" cried the blind man. Then from the parlour a voice shouted: "Bill's dead!"

"Search him!" yelled the blind man. "Get aloft and find the chest!" Feet pounded up the stairs; the window of the Captain's room was forced open. A man's head leaned out calling down to the blind man.

"Pew!" he called him. "They've been afore us! Turned the chest out!"

"Is it there?" roared Pew.

"The money's there!" came the reply.

Pew cursed them all. "Flint's papers, I mean! . . . You below there – look in Bill's pockets."

A man came to the door. "Bill's been searched a'ready – nothing left." Pew was beside himself.

"It was the inn people! They were here when I came earlier . . . had the door locked. Find 'em, all of you, find 'em!"

Then followed more banging about; furniture overturned; doors bashed in.

The low whistle came again from the hillside.

"There's the signal!" cried one. "We'll have to budge, mates." But Pew kept ordering: "Find 'em! . . . Find 'em!"

All the men were arguing while Pew bullied and cursed. "We've got the gold, Pew." They tried to calm him down but his temper rose even higher and he struck out with his stick.

Then I heard horses galloping. A pistol shot rang out from the hedge – evidently their final warning, for the men fled in all directions.

The blind man was left – alone. "Johnny! . . . Black Dog! . . . Dirk! . . . You won't leave old Pew, mates! . . . Don't leave old Pew!"

Horsemen swept by at full gallop. Pew turned and rolled into the ditch. Then he was up and making a dash for it. He was completely bewildered and ran straight into the horses.

The riders could do nothing. With a scream, Pew went down; trampled into silence.

I scrambled up the bank and hailed the men. One was Supervisor Dance with revenue officers. They'd turned out to investigate a lugger, smuggling perhaps, in the cove. On the way, they'd met the boy riding for the doctor and had brought him back.

Pew was dead.

We carried my mother to a cottage where she soon recovered. Not one of the buccaneers was caught and the lugger got away. I went back to the Admiral Benbow with Mr Dance to find our home in ruins.

"If they got the gold, what else were they after?" he asked. "Something I have in my breast pocket, sir; I'd like to hand it to Dr. Livesey."

"Quite right, Hawkins, quite right. I'll ride there myself and report Pew's death. Come along."

He had me mounted with another rider and we set off.

The Captain's papers

We found the doctor dining with Squire Trelawney. They made us welcome and listened carefully to our story.

I gave the oilskin packet to the doctor and he slipped it into his own pocket.

After Mr Dance had left, the squire looked at Dr. Livesey.

"Well?" he asked. The doctor laughed. "You've heard of this Flint, I suppose?"

"Heard of him!" repeated the squire. "He was the most bloodthirsty pirate that ever sailed!"

"Supposing," went on the doctor, pulling out the packet, "we have here a clue to Flint's buried treasure, would it be worth our while to search?"

The squire spoke earnestly: "If we fitted out a ship and you, Hawkins and I searched a whole year, it would be more than worth our while."

"Very well," said the doctor. "Now, Jim, with your permission. we'll open the packet."

He cut the stitches and out came a note-book and a sealed paper. We pored over the notes – the crosses, dates, names of places and amounts of money.

"Make anything of it?" asked the doctor."

"Yes!" answered the squire. "It's the rascal's account-book. Places they plundered – amounts due to him – values of foreign money . . . Well, well! . . . Open the paper."

The doctor opened the seal carefully. It was a map – a map of an island. Latitude, longitude, soundings, names of hills and bays – all were marked.

There were two land-locked harbours, and a hill in the centre, 'The Spy-Glass'. Three red crosses – two N. of the island and one SW. were marked. Beside this last, the words 'Bulk of treasure here,' had been written in a small neat hand. On the back of the map, in the same writing, was more information:- 'Tall tree, Spy-glass shoulder, bearing a point to the N. of NNE. Skeleton Island ESE. and by E. Ten feet.
The bar silver is in the north cache; ten fathoms S. of black crag with the face on it. Arms, in sand hill, N. point of N. inlet cape bearing E and a quarter N.'

I didn't understand it but the squire and Dr. Livesey were delighted.

"Livesey," said the squire, "give up this practice at once. Tomorrow I start for Bristol. In ten days' time we'll have a ship and a crew; Hawkins, our cabin-boy; you, the ship's doctor; I shall be the Admiral! We'll take Redruth, Joyce and Hunter my most reliable men. We'll find Flint's treasure! . . . There'll be gold enough to roll in!" The doctor laughed.

"Trelawney," he said, "I'll go with you and I dare swear Jim will too. There's only one man I'm afraid of – you! . . . You cannot hold your tongue. We aren't the only ones who know of this paper. Those wretches at the inn tonight; the others aboard that lugger – they'll be after the money too. None of us must go about alone and from this moment we must not breathe a word of what we have found."

"Livesey," replied the squire. "You are so right. I'll be as silent as the grave."

I go to Bristol

Several weeks passed before we were ready to go to sea. I stayed at the Hall in the care of Squire Trelawney's servant, Redruth. Dr. Livesey attended to business in London.

One day a letter came, 'To be opened by Redruth or young Hawkins in Dr. Livesey's absence.'
Old Anchor Inn, Bristol, March 1, 17--.
'Dear Livesey,' I read. 'I send this letter home and to London in case you are still there. The ship is bought and fitted. A splendid schooner of two hundred tons – Hispaniola. I got her through my friend, Blandly. He's been a great help. So have they all in Bristol – especially since knowing where we were sailing – for treasure, I mean.'

(So, I thought; the Squire has been talking after all. So much for his promise to keep silent as the grave!)

'Getting the crew proved more difficult until I met an old sailor, Long John Silver. He keeps a public house here – knows all the seafaring men. He lost a leg in the wars but longs to get back to sea. He offered himself as cook and in no time had a crew for me to sign on.

So, my dear Livesey, the sea and adventure await us!

Let young Hawkins visit his mother for one night, and then, both of you, come full speed to Bristol.

Blandly, by the way, will send a ship out to us if we don't return by the end of August. He's found us an admirable sailing master and John Silver came across a capable man, Arrow, for mate. We'll even have a bo's'n who pipes! What more could we want?

John Trelawney'

I was thrilled and excited. The next morning, Redruth and I set out for the Admiral Benbow. Mother was well and comfortable. The squire had had everything repaired; even an armchair put in the bar for her. A boy had been apprenticed and would help while I was away.

The following day I said goodbye to my mother, to the inn and the cove I had known all my life.

The coach picked us up and I slept most of the way. Redruth woke me with a dig in the ribs. "Come on!" he shouted, "Bristol!"

We walked along the quays past masses of ships – all sizes and from all nations. Foreign languages and cargo smells filled the air.

I almost burst with excitement. I, Jim Hawkins, was going to sea; bound for an unknown island – to search for treasure!

At the Spy-Glass Tavern

When we met Squire Trelawney, he sent me with a note for John Silver at the Spy-Glass Tavern.

An attractive place it looked, with its brass telescope for a sign, but so busy and noisy with seamen, I was almost afraid to enter. Then I saw a man with one leg, tall and strong with a pleasant, intelligent face. When I'd first read the squire's letter I'd wondered if his sailor with one leg was the man the old Captain had warned me about. Surely, that wasn't possible? Here was a smiling, respectable landlord – so different from Black Dog and the blind man, Pew.

"Mr Silver, sir?" I asked, going up to him with the note.

"Yes, my lad," he answered, and then, "Why, you must be Hawkins, our new cabin boy. Well, I'm pleased to meet you."

Just then a customer stood up quickly and hurried out of the door. I recognised him at once. "Oh," I cried, "stop him! That's Black Dog!"

"After him, Harry!" Silver called to the bar-man. "He hasn't paid . . ."

Silver turned to me. "Who did you say he was . . . Black . . . what?"

"Dog, sir," I answered. "Hasn't Mr Trelawney told you of the buccaneers? He was one of them."

"What!" cried Silver. "Ben, run and help Harry!" Then to another fellow, "Morgan, weren't you

drinking with him?'' But Morgan
denied any knowledge of the man.
  ''Black Dog,'' went on Silver
thoughtfully. ''No, I don't recall
. . . yet his face . . . yes, he used
to come with a blind beggar . . .''
''Yes!'' I cried. ''His name was
Pew!''
  ''It was!'' Silver came in, quite
excited. ''Pew! . . . For certain sure
– a proper shark he was.
Mr Trelawney would be pleased if
we caught one of the villains, eh?
. . . Ben's a good runner – he'll
catch him.''

My suspicions had been roused seeing Black Dog at the Spy-Glass. I watched Long John closely; he seemed genuine enough; or was he too clever for me?

When the men returned and were scolded for losing Black Dog, I would have sworn on the innocence of Long John Silver.

''See here, now, lad,'' he said, ''Whatever will Cap'n Trelawney think o' me? You find this rascal here in my tavern and I let him give us the slip. You're only a boy, but you're as smart as paint. I see that when you first came in. I'd have had him but for this . . . '' tapping his empty trouser-leg.

''The score!'' he yelled. ''He never paid!'' He started laughing against himself and laughed so heartily I had to join in.

We walked back together along the quay. Long John explained things about the ships and had endless stories to tell.

We found the squire with Dr. Livesey and Silver told them about Black Dog. He was exact and turned to me now and again with, ''That's how it were, weren't it, Hawkins?'' I could only agree. They thought it a pity to have lost Black Dog but complimented Silver on his efforts.

The squire called to him as he left.

''All aboard by four this afternoon.''

''Ay, ay, sir!'' cried the cook.

''Well,'' said the doctor, ''I don't usually trust your judgement but I must say, John Silver suits me.''

''A perfect find,'' declared the squire. ''Come, Jim, we'll see the ship.''

Powder and arms

The Hispaniola lay well out and as we came alongside we were met and saluted by the mate, Mr Arrow.

The captain, a sharp and angry looking man asked to see the squire immediately.

"Well, Captain Smollett, all ship shape and seaworthy?" asked the squire.

"No, sir," he answered. "I'll speak plain. I don't like this cruise or the men; and I don't like my officer." The squire was annoyed. "Perhaps, sir, you don't like the ship?"

"I can't answer for her – till she's tried," said the captain. "She seems a good craft."

Dr. Livesey asked calmly, "Captain, you say you don't like this cruise. Can you explain why?"

"I was taken on, sir, on sealed orders. Now I find that every man on board knows more than I do . . . AND," went on the captain, "I hear we're going after treasure. I don't like treasure voyages – especially when they are secret – even more especially when the secret's been blabbed."

The doctor raised his eyebrows.

"Yes, sir; blabbed . . . I don't think either of you two gentlemen know what you're at. But I'll tell you what I think . . . This voyage will become a matter of life and death."

"Maybe," replied the doctor, "but we are not as ignorant as you imagine. The crew, now, aren't they good seamen?"

"I don't like them, sir," Captain Smollett answered. "Besides, I should have chosen my own men."

"Perhaps," admitted the doctor. "And Mr Arrow – you dislike him?"

"I do, sir. I think he's a good seaman but he's too free and easy with the crew. A mate should keep to himself."

"Now," asked the doctor, "what do you want us to do?"

"Well, gentlemen, are you set on this cruise?"

"Absolutely!" the squire declared.

"Right," went on the Captain. "You've heard my view patiently. Now, for a few facts. They're putting the powder and arms for'ard. Why not under the cabin? Second point, your own men are being berthed for'ard, why not bring them here beside the cabin?"

"And?" asked Squire Trelawney.

"One more thing," said the captain. "I've heard you have a map of the island; with latitude, longitude and crosses marking the buried treasure."

"I never mentioned that!" cried the squire.

"Finally," went on Captain Smollett, "whoever has such a map he shall keep it secret – even from me and Mr Arrow." There was a pause.

"You fear mutiny?" asked Dr. Livesey.

"I didn't say that, sir. I see things that are not right. I am responsible for this ship, so I must be allowed to take every precaution: otherwise, I resign. Thank you for listening, gentlemen." With that he left the cabin.

"Well," said the doctor, "you have two honest men aboard – Silver and Smollett."

"Silver, yes," cried the squire, "but that captain! What a humbug!"

"We shall see," said the doctor quietly.

On deck, the men were already moving the arms and powder under supervision. Mr Arrow and the captain were to sleep on deck, while Redruth and I were to have berths with the doctor, squire, Hunter and Joyce. When Long John Silver came aboard he cried: "What ho! . . . What's all this?"

"Changing the powder," answered one of the men.

"Wasting time!" yelled Silver. "We'll miss the tide!"

"My orders!" rapped out Smollett and sent Silver and me below to prepare supper.

32

The voyage

That night was all work and bustle, but I enjoyed it.

Just before dawn the bo'sun piped; the captain gave brief commands and the men scrambled to their places.

"Now, Barbecue," cried one man to Silver, "give us a song – our one!" Out came the words I knew so well:

"Fifteen men on the dead man's chest . . ."
and the crew roared:

"Yo-ho-ho and a bottle of rum!"

In a second, I was back at the Admiral Benbow hearing, once more, the old buccaneer. Then we were away; the sails began to draw, the land and shipping swept by. Our voyage had begun.

The Hispaniola proved a good ship; the men were capable and

Captain Smollett knew his job. Mr Arrow, however, turned out worse than the Captain had feared. He had no authority over the men and after a few days at sea was often drunk. One dark night, with a heavy sea, he disappeared. The Captain seemed relieved. At that time, we did not suspect foul play.

We were, of course, without a mate, but Job Anderson, the bo'sun served. Mr Trelawney could take a watch in good weather, and Israel Hands the cox'n could turn his hand to anything. Israel was a close friend of Long John, or Barbecue, as the men called him. All the crew admired Barbecue and obeyed him. He had a charm about him and to me he was always kind. He'd welcome me into the galley: "Come and have a yarn, Hawkins," he'd say. "Nobody more welcome than you, my son. Here's Cap'n Flint, my parrot. I named her after the famous buccaneer."

"Pieces of eight! Pieces of eight!" screamed the bird – on and on until Silver covered her cage.

"That bird; why, she must be two hundred years old. Sailed with great pirates, she has; seen as much wickedness as the devil himself," he explained as the parrot reeled off every possible obscenity. "Innocent as a babe," he added, giving her sugar.

The squire and Smollett weren't any more friendly, although the Captain did admit the crew were behaving and that he'd taken a real fancy to the ship.

The men were treated well; double grog at the least excuse, extra good food on any man's birthday and a barrel of apples kept handy for the men to dip into as they pleased.

On the last day of our outward journey – we expected to sight the island that night – I passed by the barrel and fancied an apple. I had to dive right in to reach one off the bottom. Sitting there, feeling very tired, swaying with the ship's movement I must have dozed off. Someone woke me – someone sitting down and leaning against the barrel. I was about to climb out when Silver spoke. His first words kept me there in fear and trembling.

In the apple barrel

"No, Flint was Captain," Silver said. "I was quartermaster. The same time as I lost my leg, old Pew lost his eyes . . . Walrus; that was Flint's old ship – I've seen it fit to sink with blood and gold."

"Ah," put in another voice, "he was the best of 'em all was Flint."

"I sailed with England first," went on Silver, "then Flint; now, here, I'll soon take command. I saved three thousand all told.

Not bad – all safe in the bank. Where's England's men now? I don't know. Flint's? Why, here on board and glad to be fed. Pew spent twelve hundred in a year – finished up a beggar."

"What's the good o' saving?" asked a young seaman. "Enjoy it, I say."

"Fool's talk," cried Silver. "Now, you're young, you're as smart as paint. I see that when I first set eyes on you. I'll talk to you like a man."

I couldn't believe my ears! The old rogue was using the same words of flattery that he'd used to me.

"Gentlemen of fortune, like us," Silver went on, "they risk swinging; but when they go ashore they've hundreds in their pockets. Most use it quick, on rum and a fling. Not me! I salt it away – some here, some there."

"But," said the young man, "you'll never be able to go back to your place in Bristol after this."

"Quite right: but my old missus has collected it all in by now. The Spy-Glass is sold, lock, stock and barrel. When I get back the old girl will meet me somewhere."

"Can you trust your missus?"

"Nobody gets past John Silver, my lad. Some were afraid of Pew. Some feared Flint; but Flint himself was afraid o' me. Ah, lad, you can be sure of yourself in old John's ship."

"I wasn't too happy with this job," the lad admitted, "but now I've talked to you, John; well, here's my hand."

They shook hands, shaking the barrel as they did so.

There were footsteps – a low whistle brought another man over.

"Young Dick's with us," said Silver.

"O'course," came Israel Hands' voice. "No fool, is Dick But, look here, Barbecue: how much longer? I've 'ad enough o' Cap'n Smollett."

"Israel," said Silver, quite kindly, "your head ain't much – never was; but your ears are big enough, I reckon, so listen. You'll work hard, speak soft and keep sober till I give the word. You can bet on that, my son."

"Well, I do, don't I?" grumbled the cox'n. "But when? That's what I want to know."

"By the powers!" cried Silver, "I'll tell you when. The last moment I can; that's when! We've a first rate seaman sailing the ship. We've the squire and doctor with a map. Let them do the work. If I was sure of you lot, I'd let Smollett navigate halfway home afore I struck."

"Why, we're all good seamen aren't we?" ventured Dick.

"Foc's'le hands!" snapped Silver. "We can steer a course – who's to set it? I'd have the Cap'n get us back into the trade winds at least! Well, I'll finish with 'em at the island – soon as the cargo's loaded. Shiver me timbers, I've a faint heart sailing with the likes of you."

"Easy on, Barbecue," coaxed Israel. "We ain't crossing you."

"All this hurry, hurry," moaned Silver. "All leads to Execution Dock – that's what."

"John," came in Dick, "when we turn on them – what do we do?"

Silver chuckled. "That's right, Dick! Down to business! Death, I say! I don't want any of 'em turning up when I'm riding in my carriage. One, I claim . . . Trelawney. I'll twist his head off with these hands . . . Dick," he added, "you just dig me out an apple – there's a good lad."

I was terrified; my legs like jelly. Then Hands exclaimed: ''Oh, forget the apples, John. Let's have a go at the rum.''

''Here's the key, Dick,'' said Silver. ''I trust you; fill a pannikin and bring it up.''

While Dick was gone, Israel spoke in a whisper. ''Not another man of 'em will join us. So, there were still a few faithful ones aboard, I thought shivering.

On Dick's return each drank – ''To luck!'' . . . ''To old Flint;'' . . . ''To ourselves.''

A light fell on me; the moon had risen and at the same time the look-out shouted, ''Land-ho!''

Council of War

During the excitement and rush for the bow, I was out of the barrel, doubling back to the stern and then joining Dr Livesey and Hunter on deck. I was dazed with all I'd heard, yet through the mist I saw three hills and heard Captain Smollett giving orders. He asked if any one of them had seen that land before.

"Yes, sir," answered Silver, "the trader I was cook in – put in for water. Good anchorage behind that tiny island there – Skeleton Island. Rare place for pirates, once, sir. One of the hands knew all the names, Fore-mast Hill, Main and Mizzen. The Main, they called Spy-Glass – they kept watch from there, sir."

"Here's a chart," went on Captain Smollett. "See if that's the place."

Silver's eyes sparkled; but the paper was clean and fresh – obviously a copy with the crosses and notes left out. However disappointed he must have been, Silver managed to hide it.

"Yes, sir, this is the spot for sure. Ah, Cap'n Kidd's Anchorage, well I never, just the name my shipmate called it. A strong current runs along south, then north up the west coast. There's no better place to anchor."

I was amazed at Silver calmly admitting he knew the island and I almost shuddered as he came up and put his hand on my shoulder. "Ah, Hawkins," he said, "this is a grand place for a boy. When you want to explore, you just ask me for a snack. Why, I almost feel young again myself." He patted my shoulder and went below. As soon as I had the chance I spoke to the doctor.

"Please, sir, will you get the squire and the captain to the cabin and then send for me on some pretence – I have terrible news."

The men were cheering; for the captain had just announced "grog all round."

In a few minutes I was sent for and I found all three waiting for me.

"Now, Hawkins," said the squire. "What is it? Speak up."

I repeated everything I'd overheard. No questions were asked; they watched me closely, to the very end.

"Sit down, Jim," said the doctor kindly and gave me wine. They thanked me and drank my health.

"You were right, Captain," acknowledged the squire. "I've been a fool." "No more than I, sir," returned the captain. "But never a sign of what they were planning – it beats me."

"Silver's influence," put in the doctor, " – a most remarkable man." They discussed things and counted the men on our side. With the squire's servants we made seven. We couldn't be sure of anyone else yet. The captain thought we should carry on quite normally for the time being.

"Jim," said the doctor, "you can help more than anyone. The men talk to you and you notice things. Report anything you hear or see – anything." I left the cabin feeling very scared

My shore adventure

Next day we anchored, between the mainland and Skeleton Island. Trees grew down to high water mark and two river swamps emptied into the harbour. The heat was stifling; a stagnant smell hung over everything.

"I don't know about treasure," said the doctor, "but I guarantee fever." The men were restless and quarrelsome. The captain suggested they be given a free afternoon – to go ashore if they wished.

Hunter, Joyce and Redruth were taken into our confidence and we were issued with loaded pistols.

The men had till sundown – a gun would be fired half an hour earlier. Six would remain on board; Silver and the others started to embark on two small boats. Suddenly, I thought I would go ashore too. I was over the side and curled up in the bow of the nearest boat.

Silver must have noticed. "That you, Jim?" he called from the other boat. We beached first. I caught a branch, swung myself out and ran.

Silver shouted: "Jim! Jim!" but I was off.

The first blow

I had landed on swampy ground but soon climbed to open country with pines and mis-shapen trees, like oaks. A thicket of these spread from a sand-knoll down to the river bed.

Voices came nearer; I dived under the branches like a frightened mouse. I heard Silver and through a peep-hole saw him face to face with a man named Tom.

"Mate," he was almost pleading, "I think gold-dust o' you. Why else should I warn you, Tom, eh? I'm trying to save your neck!"

"Silver," Tom replied, "surely you've more sense than to be led by that lot o' swabs? I'd sooner lose my hand than fail my duty!"

Here was one honest man, at least. There was a noise; a cry; a long-drawn scream and Tom leapt at the sound. "What in heaven's name?" he cried.

"Reckon that was Alan," said Silver not turning a hair.

"They've killed Alan?" Tom cried. He strode back towards the beach.

Silver held onto a branch and sent his crutch hurling after Tom. It struck him to the ground and Silver reached him in a shot. Then he drove his knife, twice, into the still body. I must have fainted; the world swam and bells rang in my ears. When I came to, the monster had his crutch again.

He wiped his knife on the grass; pulled a whistle from his pocket and blew several times. Tom and Alan were dead. Would I be next?

I crawled out of the thicket and ran. On and on I went till I found myself at the foot of a small hill – it had two peaks. The trees were further apart and the air was fresh. The sound of small stones tumbling down made me turn; I stood fixed in terror.

The man of the Island

A shaggy figure sprang behind a pine. Was it bear, man or monkey? Even Silver seemed less terrifying. I turned to go back. The creature re-appeared heading me off. It darted from tree to tree, bent almost double, but on two legs and at great speed.

I almost yelled for help; then remembering my pistol walked straight towards the figure. He came out to meet me, hesitated, then threw himself down holding out his hands.

"Who are you?" I gasped.

"Ben Gunn," he croaked. "Poor Ben Gunn, I am. Haven't spoken to another Christian soul for three years." He had long hair and a beard – quite white. His skin was sun-burnt, his lips almost black. As for his clothes, he wore old bits of sail cloth held together with brass buttons, bits of stick and string.

"Three years!" I cried. "Were you shipwrecked?"

"Nay, not shipwrecked – marooned."

I had heard the word. Buccaneers would put an offender on a lonely island, and leave him to his fate.

"Marooned," he repeated. "Lived on goats, berries and oysters, I have. You don't happen to have a bit o' cheese? . . . No? . . . I dream o' cheese."

"If I ever get aboard again," I promised, "you shall have all the cheese you want."

"If?" he repeated. "Why, who's to stop you?" "Not you, for sure," I answered.

He asked my name and kept saying, 'Jim' as if he liked it. After looking round several times he said: "Jim, Jim boy, I'm rich."

I thought the poor old man was crazy.

"Rich, I says! Ah, Jim, you're lucky to be the first to find me."

He grasped my hand. "Tell me true, Jim. Is it Flint's ship?"

"No, Flint's dead," I answered, "but some of Flint's men are on board; worse luck for the rest of us."

"Not a man with one leg?" he asked.

"Yes; Silver. He's the cook and the ringleader."

Ben still gripped my hand.

"If Long John sent you, I'm just dead meat," he said. Then, on the spur of the moment, I told him everything. He listened carefully.

"You're a good lad, Jim and you're all in a clove-hitch – I'll say! Well, you just trust Ben Gunn . . . Would your squire be a fair-minded man, you reckon?"

"Most fair," I told him. "All hands are to share."

"And get a passage home?" he asked. "Of course," I declared. "Besides, if we get rid of the others we'll need you to help work the ship."

"Ah, so you would . . . I'll tell you this much . . . I was on Flint's ship when he buried the treasure – him and six strong men. A whole week ashore, he was, us standing off in the old Walrus . . . He came back alone. Billy Jones was mate and Silver quartermaster. They asked him about the treasure. He told 'em they could stay if they liked – he was off for more." Ben paused.

"Three years ago I sighted this island from another ship. I told the lads about the treasure and we searched – all no good. They turned on me then – left me with a musket, spade and a pickaxe. 'Find it yourself,' that's what they said."

Ben went on in great detail of what I should tell the squire.

"But," I broke in, "how do I get on board?"

"There's my boat – made with me own hands – under the white rock she is . . . we could try that, come dark . . . Hi!" he cried. "What's that?"

With two hours to sundown, a cannon thundered across the island.

"They're fighting!" I yelled. "Follow me!" He kept close, trotting easily and chatting. We heard shots. Then above the trees, fluttering – there waved the Union Jack.

The Doctor finds the stockade

Meanwhile, things had been happening to those on board and here I set down the story told me much later by Dr Livesey. It was about half-past one when the two boats left Hispaniola.

The captain, squire and doctor were talking in the cabin when Hunter reported that I'd gone ashore. They decided that the doctor and Hunter should go too and they pulled for the stockade marked on the map. Steering round a slight bend they were out of sight of Silver's men. There, on a small rise sat a stout log-house, fit to hold twenty, with loopholes for muskets on every side, and surrounded with a six-foot paling fence. The doctor saw a spring bubbling up and running down the slope. When he heard Alan's death scream he thought, "That was Jim," and re-joined Hunter waiting in the boat.

Back on Hispaniola the doctor suggested that the six of them should leave the ship and set themselves up in the log-house. They'd be more able to defend themselves and they'd have plenty of water. They agreed. So, while Redruth was on guard, the boat was loaded with food, liquor, arms and medicines.

The captain then hailed the cox'n. "Mr Hands," he called, "here are two of us – each armed. If you try to make a signal to your friends on shore, we'll shoot to kill.

This took the men by surprise and they kept below. Then Joyce, the doctor and Hunter made off with the stores for the log-house.

After a second load had been taken, Joyce and Hunter remained on shore while the doctor rowed back to the ship. Finally, with a musket and cutlass for each one and the rest of the arms dumped overboard, the captain, the squire, Redruth and the doctor were ready to leave.

Once more the men were hailed. "Abraham Gray!" shouted the squire. "Listen to me. I am leaving the ship. I order you to follow your captain. You're a good man at heart – come now, don't risk more lives!"

There was a scuffle; then out burst Gray with a cut across his cheek.

"I'm with you, sir!"

They shoved off – clear of the ship – but not safe yet.

At the stockade

That trip was difficult; the over-loaded boat being carried towards Silver's boats by the ebbing tide. Suddenly the captain remembered that shot and powder for the cannon hadn't been dumped – they'd forgotten!

Looking back, they saw the five rogues stripping the tarpaulin cover.

"Mr Trelawney," asked the captain, "will you pick me off one of those men? Hands, if possible."

But at that second, Hands stooped so another man was shot. His cry was echoed by the men on board and on shore.

"Tell us when the gun's about to fire," said the captain, "and we'll hold water."

"Ready!" cried the squire.

"Hold!" ordered the captain.

He and Redruth backed with a great heave – the stern was under water. The cannon shot whizzed over their heads, sinking them by the draught, but they waded out unharmed. That was the shot I heard with Ben Gunn. Several weapons were sunk with the boat and provisions.

The men made for the stockade as the buccaneers on shore raced through the trees to cut them off. Shots were fired. One enemy fell; the rest ran. Poor Redruth was severely wounded. He was carried in and the squire knelt by him

until he died.

The captain pulled a flag from his bundle of things and reverently covered the dead body.

He and Hunter fixed the trunk of a fir tree to the corner of the log-house and soon had the Union Jack flying.

More cannon balls came over but fell short. Gray and Hunter volunteered to rescue the lost provisions now that the tide was out, but Silver and his men were there first and well armed.

The captain was entering my disappearance in the log when a voice cried, "Doctor! . . . Squire! . . . Captain! . . . Hallo!"

They ran to the porch and saw me, safe and sound, climbing over the fence.

Hawkins tells of Ben Gunn

Now that the gap in the story has been filled, I pick it up from the time Ben Gunn and I saw the flag.

"There's your friends!" said Ben. "I'll be off until I get your gentleman's word. You know where to find me. And when someone comes he must carry something white – and come alone."

"You mean you have a proposition to put to the squire or the doctor?" I asked.

"Right," he answered. "And if you see Silver – you wouldn't tell of Ben Gunn? . . . No, I reckon you wouldn't . . . And, Jim, if the pirates camp ashore . . . Well, I reckon, maybe, there'd be less in the morning, eh?"

A cannon ball tore through and pitched in the sand. We took to our heels – in different directions. I crept among the shore-side trees and saw the Hispaniola; from her mast flew the Jolly Roger. The cannonade was over. Some men were smashing something on the beach – it turned out to be the small boat.

A great fire glowed near the river mouth and a boat kept coming and going between shore and ship. The men were shouting; full of rum, they sounded.

Out on a sandy spit was an isolated white rock; Ben Gunn's rock perhaps. If ever we needed his boat I'd know where to look. I thought it safe, now, to make

for the stockade and I can't tell you how glad I was to be with my friends.

I told my story; everything that had happened on shore and then I looked round at our new home – a cabin made of pine trees. Sand rained in through every chink. A metal fire-basket stood on a stone slab and above, in the roof, a square hole served as a chimney.

The spring in the porch bubbled into a basin made from a ship's iron kettle. Gray sat with his face bandaged and poor Redruth's body lay along a wall.

The doctor showed me his snuff box filled with Parmesan cheese. "Very nutritious," he said. "I'll save it for Ben Gunn."

Before supper we buried Tom Redruth and later, the three chiefs discussed our prospects. Our stores would never last out but we had two allies – rum and the climate. We could hear the men roaring and singing and the doctor reckoned that camped there, in the marsh, half at least would soon be down with fever.

I slept like a log and awoke to shouts of, "Flag o' truce!" and "Why, it's Silver himself!"

That certainly made me get up.

Silver visits the stockade

Sure enough, there in the cold mist, stood two men and Silver.

The captain ordered us to keep inside and to load all muskets.

"What do you want?" he called from the porch.

"Cap'n Silver to come aboard and make terms," one man shouted.

"Cap'n Silver! Who's he?" cried Smollett.

"Me, sir," Silver answered. "These poor lads chose me after your desertion, sir. We'll submit if we can come to terms."

"Any treachery and the Lord help you," Smollett promised.

Long John threw in his crutch, climbed the fence and jumped down. Then he was up the slope and saluting the captain.

He waited to be invited in but Smollett had him sitting in the sand and brought him to the point.

"Right, Cap'n," he said, "that was a crafty trick o' yours last night and someone pretty clever with a hand-spike. It shook us – but not twice it won't. We'll do sentry."

"Well?" said the captain, cool as cool, though he had no idea what Silver meant. I suddenly thought of Ben Gunn's words – 'less in the morning'. Had he visited the buccaneers lying drunk round their fire?

"We want the treasure," said Silver. "So, just hand over the chart. I never meant you harm anyway."

"We know exactly what you meant," said the captain, slowly filling his pipe. Silver took out his own pipe and there they sat; as good as a play it was.

"Now," started Silver, "give us the chart, stop shooting poor seamen and stoving their heads in while they sleep – you do that and you have a choice. Come aboard, once we have the treasure and we'll land you safe somewhere. Or, divide stores and stay here. I'll send the first ship I sight, to pick you up . . . I say it to all you in there . . . a handsome offer!"

"Is that all?" Smollett asked, standing up.

"My last word," Silver declared. "Refuse that and all you'll get is musket balls!"

"Now listen to me," said the captain. "If you'll come, one by one, unarmed, I'll clap each in irons and take you home for a fair trial. Otherwise, I'll send you

all to Davy Jones. You can't find the treasure; you can't fight us; you can't sail the ship. And you know it! Now, move! Get out!''

Silver's face was aflame. He struggled to get up and not one helped him. Oaths and curses poured out. Over the fence at last, he turned: ''I'll smash this place – before another hour!'' he yelled. Then, he and his men made for the wood.

The attack

The captain encouraged us, gave us our orders and prepared for the coming attack. "Hawkins," he said, "neither of us is much good at shooting; we'll load and give a hand."

The sun had risen, beating on the log-house; an hour passed. Suddenly, Joyce saw movement and fired. Shot answered shot. A rifle-ball knocked the doctor's musket to bits. Pirates leapt from the woods and over the fence like monkeys. Squire and Gray shot three; but one was up and away. Then Anderson roared and slashed at the loopholes. Another snatched Hunter's musket and bludgeoned him down. At the doorway, the doctor was attacked with a cutlass.

Smoke; flashes and shots; cries and groans filled the log-house.

"Out lads!" shouted the captain. "Fight outside! . . . Cutlasses!" The doctor slammed his assailant and sent him sprawling. I came face to face with Anderson; jumped aside and rolled down the slope. Gray was behind me, caught the bo'sun unawares and cut him down. Another fell at a loophole.

One minute they swarmed over us and the next we had beaten them off. The last pirate to get away wore, of all things, a red nightcap. Five had fallen; but the others would return.

Hunter never regained consciousness; Joyce was dead and the captain had a broken shoulder and a lung wound.

Ben Gunn's boat

The squire, the doctor and the captain talked together, then, that afternoon, the doctor took up his hat, pistols, and a cutlass. He put the chart in his pocket, a musket over his shoulder and made off north, through the trees. Gray thought he was mad; I thought he'd gone to find Ben Gunn.

I had an idea too and started putting things together; I took biscuits, pistols, powder-horn and bullets. It was Ben Gunn's boat I was after and I made a bolt for the thick wood. The sea, blue and beautiful, lay before me as I came from the trees.

Alongside Hispaniola was Silver in a small boat. His parrot screamed on his wrist and he laughed with two men leaning over the bulwarks. Then he pulled away and the men went below.

I crawled to the white rock. A goatskin tent was hidden in a deep hollow and in the tent was Ben's boat. It was lop-sided and crude – a coracle covered in goatskin with a rough, double paddle.

Sitting there, thinking, I reckoned the pirates would before long want to get on board. How, if I cut the Hispaniola adrift?

I waited for the dark. Fog gathered and the tide ebbed; I had to wade through swampy sand before I could put the coracle on the water. That coracle! She went in every direction except the one I wanted. Thanks to the tide I made the ship and when the hawser slackened cut through several strands.

I heard Hands and another, drunk and quarrelling, and by pulling myself up on a cord hanging over the ship's side, I could see them in the cabin. They were both at each other's throat – in a deadly grip. I dropped back, just in time, for the ship was moving. The strong ebb-tide had snapped the last strands of the hawser and she was away. My coracle whirled along too, tossed like a cork in the ship's wake. This was the end. How could I possibly survive?

Cold, tired and very frightened I crouched down and shut my eyes. When I opened them it was broad daylight; I had slept; I was still alive!

Ben's boat had brought me to the south-west end of the island. Silver, I remembered, had mentioned a strong current; perhaps it would carry me to North Inlet. It was useless to paddle; that upset the coracle's balance. I just kept still and watched the waves rising and falling all round me.

Hawkins - Captain of Hispaniola

Then, not half a mile away, there was the Hispaniola under sail. Her course was irregular – was anyone steering? Were they both dead? Could I save her for the captain? I risked paddling and gained on her. Then, not a hundred yards away she came round in the wind and I realised my danger. How huge she looked! She was almost on me! The bowsprit was over my head. I sprang, sending the coracle under water. With one hand I grabbed the jib-boom and my foot lodged between stay and brace. I crawled along then tumbled head first on to the deck.

There were the two men – Redcap stiff on his back, obviously dead, Israel Hands half propped up. He writhed and moaned for brandy. I found food and water for myself and brandy for him.

"Where you come from?" he asked. "I've taken possession of this ship, Mr Hands, so please regard me as your captain," I replied.

I had the Jolly Roger down and threw it overboard. He watched – sly and pretty sour.

"I don't see who's to sail this ship," he said. "You give me food and drink and tie up my wound and I'll show you how. That's fair and square, ain't it?"

We agreed. Before long Hispaniola was skimming along bound for North Inlet. Everything was fine except for the eyes of Israel Hands; they followed me everywhere. He asked me to fetch wine; it seemed he wanted me to leave deck for some reason. I did; but took my shoes off and slipped back to watch.

He crawled to the scuppers, found a blood-stained knife and hid it inside his jacket. So: I was to be his next victim.

When I brought the wine he was back in his place.

Later, he said the tide was just about right. "You take my orders, Cap'n Hawkins and we'll sail slap in." He was an excellent pilot and I obeyed promptly. We entered the estuary.

"Now, boy," said Hands, "stand by! . . . starboard a little . . . steady . . . port just a little . . . steady now, steady . . . Now, me hearty, luff!"

Hispaniola swung round and we were there!

Israel Hands

It was exciting. I quite forgot the danger I was in; that Hands meant to kill me. I was thrilled about the ship. I had brought her in; she was safe alongside the sheltered bank.

What made me turn? A feeling? A shadow moving over me? I don't know. But turn I did and there he was coming for me – with the knife.

We both cried out; I, in terror, he with a roar of fury. I leapt sideways leaving go the tiller which struck Hands across the chest. I pulled out a pistol, took aim and pulled the trigger. Not a sound; the priming was useless. What a fool I'd been not to check my weapons!

Suddenly, Hispaniola pitched. We were both down and rolling

into the scuppers. The dead man
slid after us and tangled with
Hands. I was up first, sprang for
the mizzen shrouds and rattled up
to the cross-trees. Hands aimed
his knife and it struck just below
me. That gave me a few seconds. I
changed the priming and
re-charged my other pistol. By
now, Hands was hauling himself
up – the knife in his teeth. He
came slowly; I held my breath for
his next move.

"One more step, Mr Hands, and
I'll blow your head off!"

He stopped, took out the knife
and said: "Jim, we'll have to make
a bargain. But it's hard, boy, for a
master mariner to give in to a
youngster."

That made me feel pretty cock-
a-hoop. Then his hand went back
and whizz! . . . my shoulder was
pinned to the mast. In my horror
both pistols went off and dropped
down. Hands loosened his grip,
screamed, and plunged head first
into the water. Blood rose up in
a twirling stain.

I was terrified I'd fall from
the cross-trees and join him. I
shuddered at the thought. That
shudder tore the slight flesh
wound – I was free! I pulled at
the shirt and coat and climbed
down.

I dumped the dead man
overboard. His red cap floated
while he sank down side by side
with Israel Hands.

Pieces of eight

A breeze was getting up. I did what I could to the sails but Hispaniola would have to trust to luck.

My one wish was to get to the log-house. Truant I may have been, but I'd brought back a prize – surely Captain Smollett would be pleased. I climbed over the side and down a rope to the river bank. I made for the two peaked hill. Later the moonlight helped and I was soon at the stockade. A great fire burned on the other side; I couldn't understand – it was not like the Captain to have such a fire.

I crawled to the door and snores greeted me. Everything was all right. I'd creep in and surprise them in the morning. I stumbled and a voice shrieked: ''Pieces of eight! Pieces of eight!'' On and on it went. The sleepers awoke; I was grabbed and Silver swore.

''Bring a torch, Dick,'' he said.

So, the pirates were in possession and no sign of any prisoners.

''Well, if it isn't Jim Hawkins! This beats all . . . But I see you were smart when I first set eyes on you . . . '' He'd got a pipe going and sat on a brandy cask. The parrot perched on his shoulder. ''You're a lad o' spirit, Jim, but you can't face Smollett – he's stiff on discipline. The doctor too, he's agin you . . . you'll have to join Cap'n Silver. You're

in our hands, sure enough. Take your time. Nobody's pressing you, mate.''

''If I'm to choose, I've a right to know why you're here and where my friends are,'' I said.

''Very well,'' Silver answered. ''Yesterday, Mr Hawkins, Dr Livesey came with a flag o' truce. 'The ship's gone' he says. It had too! 'Let's bargain,' he says. So, here we are; the blockhouse, stores, the lot. As for them – they've wandered off.''

He drew on his pipe. ''And don't think they want you – washed their hands, they have,'' he added.

I thought for a few seconds.

''I'm past caring,'' I said. ''You've lost everything too. Ship lost, treasure lost, men – your whole plan wrecked. And who wrecked it? . . . I did . . . I was in the apple barrel the night we sighted land. I reported all your plans. I killed Hands. I cut the ship's cable and brought her where you'll never find her. Kill me! But if you spare me, bygones are bygones and when you're in court for piracy I'll be your witness and save you from the gallows.''

They were silent, staring at me.

''Now, Mr Silver,'' I went on, ''you're the best man here, if things go wrong I'd be grateful if you'd tell the doctor what I've said.''

"I'll bear it in mind," he answered. The men were for killing me, but Silver shouted them down.

"I'm Cap'n here and you'll obey! He's more a man than any two o' you!" They talked and then filed out for a meeting. Silver whispered:

"Look here, Jim Hawkins, you're within half a plank of death, AND of torture. They're going to throw me over. But I'll stand by you – now you've spoke up. I'll save your life – you save Long John from swinging."

"What I can do, I'll do," I promised.

"I'm on squire's side now, Jim. You've got that ship safe somewhere. How, I don't know – I ask no questions." He drew himself brandy.

"Jim," he asked, watching me, "why did the doctor give me the chart?" My face must have shown my utter amazement for he seemed satisfied that I knew nothing. "Some meaning there, Jim, good or bad."

The black spot again

The men returned and one passed something to Silver.

"Ah, the black spot," he remarked. "Where might you have found paper? . . . By the powers! It's cut from a Bible. You'll all swing now. What soft lubber cut a Bible?"

"Dick!" they answered.

"He'd best get to his prayers, then."

"Come on, Long John," one man interrupted. "Read what the council says."

"Right, George! . . . ah, 'Deposed' – so, that's it . . . now, let's hear your grievances and then I'll reply."

George began, "First, you've made a hash of this cruise. Second, you've let the enemy escape. They wanted to go; why? Third, you wouldn't let us go after 'em. And now, there's the boy."

"Is that all?" Silver asked quietly. "Now, I made a hash of it, eh? You all know what I planned, but that was thrown aside. Who forced my hand the very day we landed? Why, Anderson, Hands and you, George Merry. And you set yourself up as Cap'n! Well, that tops everything!"

Silver's words were sinking in.

"It's thanks to you we're so near the gibbet. Seen 'em have you? Bodies swinging; birds pecking? . . . Point four. Isn't the boy a hostage? Kill a hostage? Not me, mates! He might be our last chance. Point three. Is it nothing to have a real doctor visit you every day? You, John with your head broke? Or you, George, with the shivers and eyes the colour o' lemons?

By the way, did you know another ship was a coming? Ah! We'll see who's glad of a hostage then, eh? Point two. I made a bargain. Why? Take a look at that!''

He threw down a piece of paper – the yellow chart I'd found in the old seaman's chest. They gazed, then leapt at it, almost tearing it apart.

''Very pretty,'' said George. ''But how do we get away – with no ship?''

Silver turned on him. ''You tell me! You lost the ship: I found the treasure. Who's the better man? By the powers! I resign! Elect your new captain! I'm done with it.''

''Silver,'' they cried. ''Barbecue! . . . We'll have Barbecue!''

''So,'' said the cook calmly, ''you'll have to wait another turn, George . . . Pity, Dick spoilt his Bible.'' That was it – we settled down to sleep.

On parole

We were awakened by a clear voice: "Blockhouse ahoy! Here's the doctor!" I was glad to hear him but ashamed to look him in the face.

"Top o' the morning, doctor!" called Silver. "A surprise for you! A stranger here – fit as a fiddle!"

"Not Jim?" he asked. "Well, well . . . let's see the patients first."

He gave me a nod and went round the men. He spoke to each one and asked if they'd taken the medicine.

"Now, I should like a talk with the boy, please."

"Thought you might, doctor," said Silver. "Now, Hawkins, will you give your word of honour that you won't slip off?" I gave it, readily.

"Then, doctor," said Silver, "you just step outside the stockade and I'll bring the boy down." The men disapproved but Silver controlled them.

"Can't afford to break the treaty now," he said, waving the chart at them. We went down to the fence.

"Make a note of this, doctor," he said. "The boy will tell you I saved his life. Give me a bit of hope, sir."

"Why, John you're not afraid?" asked the doctor.

"I'm no coward, doctor – well, not so much, but I dread the gallows. You're a fair man. Remember the good I've done as well as the bad." He sat away from us on a tree stump.

"So, Jim," began the doctor sadly, "here you are. I don't blame you, but to go when Captain Smollett was ill – that was downright cowardly."

I was very upset. "Yes, doctor, I've blamed myself. My life's forfeit anyway, I'd be dead now, but for Silver. I can die . . . but if they torture me . . ."

"Jim," the doctor spoke urgently, "we can't have that. Whip over and we'll make a run for it."

"No, sir. I gave my word. You wouldn't break yours. Silver trusts me . . . But if they do use torture, I might let slip where the ship is; she lies in North Inlet."

"The ship!" he exclaimed.

I told him all that had happened.

"It seems, Jim, you are always the one to save our lives. We won't let you lose yours." He called Silver: "A piece of advice," he said. "Don't be in a hurry to look for that treasure."

"Why, sir, I can only save mine and the boy's life by searching."

"Look out for squalls, then!" warned the doctor.

"It's too much, sir!" Silver exploded. "I've done your bidding with me eyes shut. Tell me what you mean!"

"I can't," said the doctor. "It's not my secret. But, if we both get out of this, I'll do my best to save you – short of perjury."

Silver's face was radiant. "You couldn't say more, sir!"

"Now," went on the doctor, "keep the boy beside you. Shout if you need help. Goodbye, Jim."

The treasure hunt

Silver turned to me. "Jim, if I saved your life, you certainly saved mine; I'll not forget. I seen the doctor waving you over – I did. And I seen you say no . . . It seems we've to hunt under sealed orders . . . I don't like it."
We sat eating our breakfast.

"Well, mates," said Silver, "they've got the ship all right. Soon as we've got the treasure, we'll find it. As for our hostage – that's his last talk with his friends. I'll take him in line when we go hunting – keep him close. But once aboard, we'll soon settle Mr Hawkins!"

I was miserable. Silver was keeping a foot in both camps.

We set out; everybody armed except me. Silver had two guns, a cutlass at his wrist and a pistol in each pocket. Cap'n Flint perched on his shoulder. I was led along like a dancing bear. Some men carried picks and shovels, others were loaded with food and drink. We took the boats to the second river's mouth and began climbing the slope. One man started shouting, calling the others. There at the foot of a pine tree lay a human skeleton – straight, with arms up-stretched.

The men stood silent; gazing at the white bones and skull. This seemed to be grinning as it looked up at them from empty eye-sockets. Weeds grew through the ribs, between the fingers and toes; a grim spectre.

All the pleasure in their hunt drained away. Here was an omen – an omen of death. That's how they would finish up – and before how long? Silver showed no feelings. "Strange position," he said. "Look, there's Skeleton Island. Take a bearing . . . Yes! It's a pointer. One o' Flint's jokes. That's the way, mates! It's pointing the way!"

They spoke of Flint as if he were still around and singing his "Fifteen men on the dead man's chest."

"Come on," said Silver, "he's dead!"

But the pirates were still afraid of the old buccaneer.

The voice in the trees

At the top of the plateau we sat down. "There," said Silver, "three tall trees. It's child play now. Let's eat."

Suddenly from out of the trees came a voice:

'Fifteen men on the dead man's chest'

The men were shattered. They clung to one another. One leapt up. Morgan grovelled. The song stopped.

"By the powers," said Silver, struggling to speak, "It's someone sky-larking – someone of flesh and blood."

They looked to him longing to believe him. The voice broke out again:

'Darby M'Graw! . . . Darby M'Graw!'

Then with a great oath, the voice called:

'Fetch the rum, Darby!'

The pirates couldn't move. They remained fixed long after the voice had faded.

"Those were Flynn's last words," said Morgan.

"Let's go!" gasped one.

Silver would not be beaten. "I've come to get the gold, mates. Thousands – just a quarter of a mile away. I was never afraid of Flint alive. Nor, by thunder, am I afraid of him dead."

"Don't defy a spirit, John," warned Merry.

"Spirit?" said Silver. "I heard an echo. Do spirits have an echo?"

George took heart. "John's right! Come to think – that voice was more like . . ."

"Ben Gunn's!" roared Silver.

"He's dead too," came in Dick. Someone laughed.

"But nobody's afraid o' Ben Gunn – dead OR alive!" cried Merry. That restored them and they set out again.

The first and second trees were the wrong bearing. The third towered above them all. Was that the one guarding the treasure? As we came nearer, Merry shouted: "Now, mates, now!" And they ran. Suddenly they stopped dead. Silver and I joined them and we just stood and stared.

Before us gaped a great hole – dug out – with fallen sides and a growth of weeds. There was a broken pick and an old packing case bearing the name WALRUS . . . the name of Flint's ship. We'd found the place: the treasure had gone!

No longer a Chieftain

The men were dumb. Silver kept a clear head and changed his tactics in a flash. "Jim," he whispered, "take this and watch out." He passed me a pistol and edged northward. The hollow was now between us and the men. They leapt into the pit, cursing and crying. They pulled things aside and dug with their hands. Morgan yelled; he'd found a gold piece.

"Made a bargain, did you?" cried Merry. "You've tricked us all along!"

"Dig on, boys!" cried Silver. "Maybe you'll find some pig-nuts."

Merry screamed with rage, "You knew! You knew!"

Silver smirked, "Standing for Cap'n again, George?" They started scrambling out – all on the far side.

Silver kept cool as ever. He'd got courage all right.

"There's just the two of them," cried Merry, " – a cripple and a whipper-snapper! . . . Are you ready, mates? Let's finish them orf!"

He raised his arm and was about to charge when crack! crack! – musket shots rang out. Merry fell into the dip; John spun round and lay dead; the other three took to their heels. In a wink, Silver fired into Merry's struggling body. ''That's settled you, George.'' Dr Livesey, Gray and Ben Gunn were running towards us.

''Head them off the boats!'' shouted the doctor. We set off at a tremendous pace. From the brow of the slope we saw the men heading in the wrong direction so we flopped down to get our breath.

Silver joined us. ''Thank you, doctor. Just in the nick o' time you were . . . And you, Ben Gunn! Well, well. Who'd a thought you'd get the better of Long John.'' Ben was grinning and squirming with delight and embarrassment.

On our way to the boats the doctor filled in the story. Ben had found the treasure and over the years had carried it to his cave. Knowing Ben's secret and seeing no ship, the doctor went to Silver. He gave him the chart, which was useless, and the stores, for Ben had plenty on higher ground – away from malaria and nearer the treasure. When he'd seen me with Silver he hurried back to tell the others. Then, the squire was to guard the captain while he, Gray and Gunn took up positions in the pines. It was Ben's idea to use the ghost voice.

''Lucky I had young Jim with me,'' said Silver, ''you three would have cut me to ribbons – and not a thought.''

''Not a thought!'' laughed the doctor.

On reaching the boats, we smashed one and set off in the other for North Inlet.

As we entered the estuary who should come cruising towards us but Hispaniola herself! The tide had lifted her; we were just in time. We left her made secure in shallow water and went on to Rum Cove, quite near to Ben's cave. Gray was to guard Hispaniola. Squire greeted me kindly but at Silver's polite salute he boiled over.

''You're an unqualified villain, John Silver! I'm not to prosecute you, apparently. But the dead will always be hanging round your neck!''

John saluted again, ''Thank you, sir.''

''Don't you dare thank me for neglecting my duty!'' cried Trelawney.

We followed him into Ben's cave; cool it was, with a spring and pool and smooth sandy floor. Captain Smollett lay by a fire and in a far corner. shining in the firelight were great heaps of gold.

Flint's treasure. How many lives had it cost?

"Hallo there, Jim," welcomed the Captain. "You're a good lad! And you, John Silver, what brings you here?"

"Reporting for duty, sir," he replied, quick as thought.

What a feast we had that night. Silver ate with appetite and was always up and willing to serve. He was the same charming man of the outward voyage.

Homeward bound

Next morning we began transporting the gold and throughout had no trouble from the other three men.

After three days the cargo was safely stowed. That evening we heard shrieks and singing from the buccaneers. Silver said they were drunk but the doctor thought they might be raving with fever. He wanted to take them medicine. "Beggin' your pardon, sir," Silver suggested, "that would be most unwise. You'd lose your life — that's for sure."

Soon we set sail under the flag Captain Smollett had flown from the log-house. The three men must have been watching for as we came through the narrows, they were kneeling on the sand spit imploring us to take them on board. It was terrible but we couldn't risk another mutiny.

The doctor hailed them and told them where to find the stores we'd left behind. When they saw the ship steady on her course, they sent musket shots after us. We steered for the nearest South American port and the doctor and squire took me ashore. On our return, Ben Gunn had a tale to tell. Silver had gone. Ben confessed he'd helped him; but only to ensure our safety. Nobody, he reckoned, was safe with that one-legged man aboard.

So, Long John had made it — and with a considerable prize, for he'd cut through to the treasure and helped himself to a sack of coins!

We took on more seamen and made a good cruise back to Bristol before Mr Blandly had fitted out the consort. Each of us had a share of the treasure. Captain Smollett recovered and retired. Gray made good use of his money: he rose to be mate and part owner of a full-rigged ship. Poor old Ben spent or lost his fortune in a matter of days. Now he keeps a lodge and sings in church on Sundays.

Silver was never heard of again. Perhaps his wife re-joined him and they live in comfort with Cap'n Flint, the parrot.

As for me, I'm happy to be home. In my dreams I re-live the horrors of our adventure: Tom's death: the battle in the stockade: my lonely voyage in the coracle and the eyes of Israel Hands. When I wake to the parrot screaming, "Pieces of eight! . . . Pieces of eight!" I am thankful I'm not there and need never return to Treasure Island.